# Great-Grandma Tells of Threshing Day

# Great-Grandma Tells of Threshing Day

Verda Cross

Illustrations by **Gail Owens**

Albert Whitman & Company • Morton Grove, Illinois

To my sister Berniece Rabe, who
encouraged me to write.  V.C.

I wish to thank the following people
and organizations for information
they shared about early twentieth cen-
tury farming methods and machinery
in conversations and through their
exhibitions and publications:
Archie Hubbard, founder of Eastern
Fayette Guilford Museum in Guilford,
NY; Marge Jensen, secretary of the
New York Steam Engine Association
in Canandaigua, NY; The Rough and
Tumble Engineers in Kinzers, PA; and
Stemgas Publishing Company in
Lancaster, PA. Thanks, also, to J. Hayes
and his beautiful Belgians, Rose and
Jim. And special thanks to
Thomas Geoly.  G.O.

"Grandma, tell us a story about the olden days," we children would plead each summer when we went to visit Great-Grandma Swift. "Tell us about threshing day," I would add, for that was my favorite story.

Rocking gently back and forth in the high-backed rocker, Great-Grandma got a faraway look in her eyes. We children leaned forward in anticipation. Then she would begin.

Right after breakfast, I saw the steam engine come chugging down the road, with Mr. Snider steering it. Behind the engine was the big threshing machine. And behind the thresher was the water wagon, pulled by a team of horses and driven by Mrs. Snider and her son.

"Come on!" I yelled to Robbie, even though the threshing rig was a long way off.

Robbie came running out to the road. He had never seen a steam engine before. "Why aren't horses pulling the thresher?" he asked.

Father had just driven up in our wagon and was roping the horses' bridles to a tree in our yard. He laughed. "It doesn't need horses, Robbie. The steam engine pulls it. Mr. Snider is just guiding the engine—he's on a platform behind the firebox."

Father had been to the ice man and brought home a big chunk of ice. "Laura, put the washtub under the tree while I unload the ice," he called. "We'll need every bit before the day is out."

He put the ice in the tub I had ready. I wrapped it well in a piece of oilcloth and some old quilts to keep it from melting too fast. The ice would be used for lemonade and iced tea. Ice wasn't delivered in the country, so we had no icebox. We kept things cool by putting them in a milk trough filled with water.

"It's here!" Robbie yelled. "The threshing machine's here!" His voice was almost lost in the noise.

He ran to open the gates so Mr. Snider could drive into the field next to the barn. Father was busy with the horses. They reared up and tugged at their ropes when they saw the thresher and heard the noise of the steam engine, but they couldn't get away. Father spoke to them quietly, and they soon lost their fear.

It was the last of June, and in Missouri, the winter wheat was ready for harvest. Robbie and I had waited a long time for threshing day. I remembered when Father had planted the wheat in the fall. It had grown a little before the cold weather set in, and then it had come up slowly all winter under the snow. In spring, it had turned dark green and shot up fast. By the middle of June, the leaves were golden, and the grain was plump and brown.

Two weeks before, Father had cut and tied the wheat into bundles. We called them sheaves. They were tied by a special machine called a binder. We walked behind the binder with two neighbor men while they set the sheaves in stacks called shocks.

Robbie and I helped. We made sure the shocks stood up and were capped properly so the rain would drain off.

If we did it wrong, the kernels would get wet and sprout. We did it right.

The wheat could only be cut after the morning dew had dried and before the evening dew began, so it took two days to cut and bind twelve acres. The shocks standing in the field looked like tidy straw houses on a green lawn. But the lawn was clover, not grass. Father had scattered clover seed in the wheat while it was covered with snow, and now the clover was around four inches high. It would keep growing and provide two cuttings of clover hay for the livestock, with some left to sell.

The sun shone on the shocks for a few days until the kernels became dry and hard. We checked them with our thumbnails every day. One night we told Father the wheat was ready for threshing. Father agreed.

Threshing day was hot and clear. Neighbors came from all directions, driving horses hitched to big wagons. The men would help Father in the field. They wore their field clothes—bib overalls and work shirts. The women wore long dresses covered by their best print aprons. All morning long they would help Mother cook dinner. Robbie and I were to help in the kitchen, too.

It was like a holiday for the women. Although they had come to help, they would enjoy visiting as they worked. Their babies and very small children had been left at home with grandmas or older brothers and sisters who would watch them and also do the morning chores. Grandpa Greene had promised to drive around at noon and pick up all the children and babysitters so they could have a good dinner with us.

About nine o'clock, when the dew was off, the steam engine gave its first sharp whistle of the day. It was time for the threshing to begin!

Some of the women had brought pies—apple or raisin—or berry cobbler. Others had brought delicious cakes—chocolate, coconut, or molasses gingercake. It made us hungry just carrying those pies and cakes to the pie safe—that was the wooden cabinet where they would be kept cool and safe from flies. But we couldn't even have a little taste until dinner. Mother's orders.

Robbie and I helped Mother make a huge churnful of lemonade. We brought cool water from the pump house. Before we sliced the lemons, we rolled them to make them soft and juicy and to make the oil come out of the peel. Robbie poured the sugar, a cupful at a time, while I stirred with a long wooden paddle. Then we added ice. The wonderful smell had us dying of thirst. But we took only a few tastes to see if it was sweet enough. The men were to have the treat first—Mother's orders!

The day grew hotter. The men had taken a keg of water wrapped in a wet burlap sack to keep it cool. By now that water would be gone.

We carried jugs of lemonade to the threshing crew. The men working around the thresher were covered with wheat chaff—little bits of dry wheat leaves and hulls—and it even got up their noses. Some men wore red or blue print handkerchiefs over their faces. But they pulled those handkerchiefs down, wiped their mouths clean, and turned up that jug.

We watched their Adam's apples bounce as the men took big gulps of our good lemonade. They thanked us. They said they were so thirsty that the threshing would have come to a screeching stop if we hadn't brought them such a nice drink.

At last it was Robbie's and my turn. We hardly ever got lemonade because lemons were so expensive, and we loved the sweet, puckery taste. I held up that jug while Robbie drank, and then he held it for me. Oh, it was good!

We stayed for awhile to watch before going back to help Mother.

The work was done in an orderly manner. Three teams were busy hauling sheaves to the thresher. Each team pulled a wagon slowly along from shock to shock. Two men on foot used pitchforks to load the golden wheat sheaves onto the wagon. When the wagon was piled high, it was driven to the threshing machine, which stayed in one place all day. While one wagon was at the thresher, another was in the field, and the third was pulling in.

At the thresher, men stood on the piled wheat and pitched sheaves into the machine. There the stalks and husks—the straw—were separated from the grain. The clean grain poured out of a metal tube and flowed into sacks. Father sewed the filled sacks shut using a slightly curved needle and heavy twine.

Two more men loaded the sacks onto another wagon waiting to go to the mill. While one wagon was being loaded, a second was at the mill, and a third was on its way back.

The straw blown from the thresher went through another big tube onto the straw stack several feet away. Throughout the day, the stack would get higher and higher. Father said it would be a mountain by sundown. Robbie and I made plans for sliding down that mountain.

About eleven o'clock, Mother said it was time to set up tables under the trees in the front yard. Father had already set the huge sliding door from the barn on some wooden horses. Robbie and I spread the barn door with freshly laundered sheets. I yelled to Robbie, "Don't pull your end down so far!" He yelled back, "Why don't you hold onto your end better!"

Then two women helped Robbie and me move the dining-room table outside. I carried the extra leaves. We put Mother's best tablecloth on this table.

There still weren't enough places for people to sit. So Robbie helped drive some wooden stakes into the ground, and I helped the women lift two of our closet doors off their hinges. We carried the doors outside, put them on the stake legs, and covered them with two more big sheets.

And then we started carrying out the food! Soon every table was laden, thanks to Robbie's and my help.

Promptly at eleven-thirty, the steam engine gave a blast to signal time out for dinner. The men came in from the field and eyed the dinner as they marched by with their horses. We had a hand pump and a watering trough in our backyard. I liked to watch the horses drink and snort and blow waves on the water. And it was fun to watch the men wash up. They cupped their hands and splashed water onto their faces, laughing and joking all the while. Some men even stuck their heads under the water flow while their friends pumped. They dried themselves with the towels Robbie and I had hung from our mulberry tree. Then they were ready to eat.

The women stood proudly by the tables, waving tree branches to keep flies away from the food. Even on an ordinary day, a farmer's biggest meal comes at noon. But this dinner was extraordinary!

There was a huge roast beef, fried chicken, slices of fried ham, chicken and dumplings, mashed potatoes, gravy, sauerkraut and weiners, fried okra, green beans, corn on the cob, sliced tomatoes, green peppers, pickles, coleslaw, potato salad, fruit salad, wilted onions, lettuce and radishes, baked beans, bean soup, fried sweet potatoes, fresh cornbread, and light bread. For dessert there was bread pudding and all those wonderful pies and cakes that the women had brought, plus three custard pies Mother had made.

Even though we had worked very hard, Robbie and I had to wait for the men to eat first. Mother's orders.

I was in charge of pouring the drinks. There was a big pitcher of our lemonade, fresh cold buttermilk, coffee, iced tea, and water. I used a metal dipper, and Mother said I did a fine job.

Robbie got to cut the pies with his pocketknife. Mother said he did a fine job, too, but when I went to tell him, he had disappeared. Then I was too busy pouring more drinks to run around looking for him.

After the men had second and even third helpings of everything, they left again for the field. The back-to-work whistle sounded just as Grandpa Greene drove up with several grandmas and nearly two dozen children on his old hay wagon. They were all hungry.

It was time for Robbie and me to eat, too. I thought I'd better find him before all the food was gone. I looked and looked, and there he was, under a table. He had snuck a raisin pie and eaten the whole thing.

"You're going to be sick," I told him.

"Just leave me be," he said.

It didn't look as if Robbie was going to eat any more, so I hurried to join the other children around the big barn-door table.

I was sorry that Robbie missed out on all that good eating. I had some of everything, and it was scrumptious! Nothing ever tastes as good as dinner on threshing day.

As soon as the children had been served, the women sat down. They ate and laughed and visited for a long time.

After dinner, we girls helped the women clean up while the boys watched the threshers. Someday, they would be in charge of threshing day on their own farms, and they needed to know how to do things. Then Grandpa Greene took the women and children home so they could start the evening chores.

Around three o'clock, Robbie's stomach was settled, and off we went again with our lemonade jugs to the thirsty threshing crew. The straw stack had grown into a great golden mountain. Father said we'd have to wait until it settled enough so we could slide along on the top straw and not fall inside. We tested it, anyway, and sunk in up to our knees. We agreed it wasn't ready for sliding yet.

So we chased rabbits.

We found some killdeer eggs.

We rode on the water wagon when Mrs. Snider and her son fetched more water and wood for the steam engine. We felt the heat of the blaze as Mr. Snider stoked the burner. Most of the men only stood by the hot engine a short while, but Mr. Snider had to stay there all day.

We ran home and rested in the cool shade of the mulberry tree.

We decided that all the men needed more ice-cold lemonade, so we took them some a second time that afternoon, and I carried along a tin of cookies. The men said we made the best lemonade of anybody and that the cookies were the best they'd ever eaten. Father said we were pretty good helpers, all right. He was mighty proud of us.

Mother came out with three empty mattress ticks—mine, Robbie's, and our parents' big one. We helped her fill them with the straw. One of the men hauled them to the back door for us.

By the time the sun had grown to a big red ball in the western sky, the very last of the shocks had been gathered. Father fed the big threshing machine its last load. Then came the fourth and final long, shrill blast from the steam whistle. The work was done!

All the men returned to their own farms, and the Sniders drove their threshing rig back down the road.

Robbie and I helped with evening chores. While I fed the chickens and gathered the eggs and made sure to fasten the henhouse door, Robbie helped Father feed the horses and cow, pump water, and carry in wood. Mother milked the cow, strained the milk into crocks, and put them in the milk trough to cool.

Supper was extra nice because we had all the good leftovers. It was Robbie's first chance at things, and he was very happy. But he didn't eat any pie.

After supper, Robbie took a bath on the back porch in the largest washtub, in water that had been warming in the sun most of the afternoon. When he came in, dressed in his nightshirt, I took my turn in the tub.

"We'll be helping Mr. Apple with his wheat tomorrow," Father said, "but at least I won't have to wake up the ice man before breakfast."

The moon came up very bright. It was time for one last look out the window at the big golden straw stack in our field. "I'm naming that stack Yellow Mountain," I told Mother, "and I'm going mountain climbing real soon."

"Allow about six weeks for it to settle," Mother said, shoving each of us toward the stairs. "You two have had enough for today. Into bed, now, and that's an order!"

We obeyed. I said my prayer of thanks for the day, folded back the patchwork quilt, climbed into my very high bed between soft cotton sheets, and settled into the sweet, fragrant comfort of the newly filled tick mattress.

"Threshing day is the best day of the year!" Robbie called to me from his room.

"I'll remember it all the days of my life," I called back to my brother.

*"And I did just that," Great-Grandma said.*

*Verda Cross* was born on a farm near
Dexter, Missouri, in 1914. She was the sixth
child in a family of thirteen children. Her
formal education stopped after tenth grade,
when her mother died. Verda married at
sixteen, raised two sons, and was a grandmother
when she was thirty-four. She and her husband
ran a farm and later a mobile home park. At
fifty-five, Verda went back to school and became
a Licensed Practical Nurse.

All her life, Verda has written stories and
poems for the children in her family. This is
her first published book.

*Gail Owens* has illustrated numerous books
for children, including I'M THE BIG SISTER
NOW by Michelle Emmert.

The text typeface is Goudy Normal.
The illustrations were done in pastel.
Designed by Karen Johnson Campbell.

Library of Congress Cataloging-in-Publication Data

Cross, Verda.
  Great-grandma tells of threshing day /
Verda Cross; pictures by Gail Owens.
    p. cm.
  Summary: A little girl and her brother help
out on threshing day in the early 1900s as the
neighbor men arrive to thresh the family's wheat
and bring it to the mill, and the neighbor women
assist with the huge midday meal.
  ISBN 0-8075-3042-5
  [1. Wheat—Threshing—Fiction. 2. Farm
life—Fiction.] I. Owens, Gail, ill. II. Title.
PZ7.C88276Gr          1992              90-28442
[Fic]—dc20                                  CIP
                                              AC

Text © 1992 by Verda Cross.
Illustrations © 1992 by Gail Owens.
Published in 1992 by Albert Whitman & Company,
6340 Oakton Street, Morton Grove, Illinois 60053-2723.
Published simultaneously in Canada
by General Publishing, Limited, Toronto.
All rights reserved. Printed in the U.S.A.
10 9 8 7 6 5 4 3 2 1